LOVE IN A POOL

by Robert Reichert

Adapted from a story
by Théophile Gautier

LOVE IN A POOL

GREEN TIGER PRESS / *Published by Simon & Schuster*
New York London Toronto Sydney Tokyo Singapore

GREEN TIGER PRESS
Simon & Schuster Building
Rockefeller Center
1230 Avenue of the Americas
New York, New York 10020

GREEN TIGER PRESS is an imprint of
Simon & Schuster Inc.

Designed by Joy Chu
The text of this book is set in
Administer Light.
The illustrations were done in watercolor
on D'Arches cold press paper.
Manufactured in the United States of America
10 9 8 7 6 5 4 3 2 1

Library of Congress Cataloging-in-Publication Data
Reichert, Robert.
Love in a pool / by Robert Reichert.
p.   om.
Summary: Two beaver friends quarrel,
causing a rift which lasts
for years until a potential tragedy
reunites them.
[1. Beavers—Fiction.   2. Friendship—Fiction.]
I. Title.   PZ7.R2643Lo 1991
[Fic]—dc20   90-85017
                    CIP

ISBN: 0-671-74788-6

To Lorna

O

n a calm, clear pond nestled in the woods lived two beavers, Shagbark and Cattail. They had been friends for as long as either could remember. As kits, they paddled happily through the forest streams, stopping to nibble on juicy birch bark or fleeing the scent of the hungry otter. Their fur grew thick, their bodies stout, and their teeth long and sharp.

The friends were alike in every way but one: Shagbark loved to talk and he chattered like dry leaves on a windy day. Cattail, on the other hand, was as silent as a snowflake.

When the time came to find mates and raise their families, the beavers built two fine huts of mud and sticks, one on either side of the pond.

"We will be neighbors forever!" Shagbark exclaimed when their lodges were complete. "No one could ask for a better home than this!" Cattail smiled, thinking of happy times ahead.

The two friends enjoyed their busy, peaceful lives, until the day of their great quarrel.

One autumn morning, the mist rising off the water revealed a world of crimson and gold. The forest rang with the sound of falling trees as Shagbark and Cattail prepared for the harsh winter. Dams needed to be repaired, food stored, and the huts made tight and cozy.

They worked for what seemed to be forever, but neither would admit that he was tired.

"You're lucky that you have me for a friend, Cattail." Shagbark said, grumpy with fatigue. "As slow as you are, you wouldn't finish anything before winter."

Now in truth, Cattail did most of the work while Shagbark gave orders left and right. The good natured fellow had long ago grown used to his friend's work habits, but this morning he lost his temper.

"If your talk could bring down trees the dam would have been finished long ago," he declared angrily.

"What?" snapped Shagbark feeling terribly hurt. "If I wasn't always telling you where to gnaw, many branches would have fallen on your empty head by this time!"

Suddenly a lifetime of good feelings were forgotten, and anger ruled the pond.

From their unkind words grew an awful separation. Shagbark and Cattail determined to build a wall through the middle of the pond, dividing their homes forever.

"I'll show him who talks too much!" muttered Shagbark, chewing furiously on a tree branch.

"I'll show him whose head is empty!" spluttered Cattail from the opposite shore.

The former friends had never worked so hard before.

At last the wall was finished. Covered with snow and icicles it rose high into the air. Winter had come and Shagbark and Cattail were not ready for it. They had been far too busy with their feud to remember the long, frozen months ahead.

Shagbark sat alone, gazing sadly at the wall. For a moment, he wished that it would melt away, as if in a dream.

As the years passed, the wall became overgrown with thornbushes and brambles. Many kits were raised in its shadow and taught by Shagbark and his mate, Hickory, to fear anything beyond it. Cattail was never seen or heard. Perhaps he no longer lived on the pond? It was sad to remember.

Like a clinging vine, the old feud had twisted itself around Shagbark's family and grown up with it.

Early one spring, Marsh was born. As the days moved into summer, she explored the wonders of the pond with a special eagerness.

"She's a curious one," Shagbark said proudly to Hickory, watching Marsh paddle in the rosy twilight.

Insects hummed and darted wildly, racing each other through the thick rays of the setting sun.

Marsh longed to know what lay beyond the mysterious wall. One evening she decided to find out. Shagbark and Hickory were off foraging in the deep woods and would not return for hours. A blackbird scolded loudly, as if warning Marsh to turn back.

Peeking through a gap in the wall, Marsh saw a perfect upside-down version of her own world reflected in the glass-smooth surface of the pond.

A leaping fish rippled the still water, making a circle which soon disappeared.

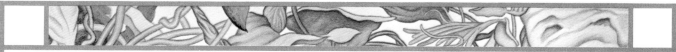

All at once, Marsh noticed a reflection on the water that was not her own. A face took shape in the blue of the pond. It seemed to look at her with sparkling eyes. The gleaming vision smiled and the beat of her heart quickened. A soft wind sang in the reeds.

Marsh knew that the figure mirrored in the pool could not be the danger about which her father had warned.

Day after day, Marsh returned to the enchanted spot. She was there in the wild, fragrant morning and when the night was mysterious and dark. Shy whispers passed through the wall and she learned that her new friend was Alder and that he was the son of Cattail. The ancient quarrel stood between them.

One night, in the light and silence of the full moon, Alder began to climb the wall. On the other side, Marsh heard the faint sound of cracking branches rising above the water. The air smelled dangerous and new.

Suddenly, a giant portion of the wall caved in with a loud roar and sank helplessly into the pond.

Marsh looked around frantically, but there was no sign of Alder. A cold breeze sent shivers through the rippling water.

From out of the shadows Shagbark appeared. Another stood by his side. It was Cattail.

The two silhouettes faced each other in silence. Then, in one motion, they dove into the pond.

Shagbark and Cattail searched the wreckage for Alder. They worked together as they had in the old days and soon managed to free him from the tangled trap of the fallen wall. Marsh watched gratefully as they brought her friend safely to shore where they were united at last.

A mist of happy tears hung over the pond, and Shagbark and Cattail felt ashamed of their stupid feud.

"Our pond which we foolishly divided knows love again," exclaimed the enlightened Cattail.

Shagbark only nodded his head. For once, he had nothing to say.

Shagbark and Cattail worked hard in the days that followed and the great wall vanished from the water.

Marsh and Alder realized their wish to know each other and found that the heart is a pond that has neither shores nor bottom.

As time went by, the bright colors of the spring flowers, the shadows of the autumn clouds, and many things besides, were reflected in the still, smooth surface of the pool.